Marpel Is Stuck!

And Other Really Good Reasons to FORGIVE

Chariot Victor Publishing
A Division of Cook Communications

Written and illustrated by
Sandy Silverthorne

To Christy:
You are truly a gift from God.

Chariot Victor Publishing
a division of Cook Communications,
Colorado Springs, Colorado 80918
Cook Communications, Paris, Ontario
Kingsway Communications, Eastbourne, England

MARPEL IS STUCK!
© 1999 by Sandy Silverthorne for text and illustrations

Designed by Keith Sherrer
Edited by Kathy Davis

First hardcover printing, 1999
Printed in the United States of America
03 02 01 00 99   5 4 3 2 1

Library of Congress Cataloging-in-Publication Data

Silverthorne, Sandy, 1951-
        Marpel is stuck! : and other really good reasons to forgive /
by Sandy Silverthorne.
            p.   cm.
        Summary: Marpel plans revenge when she does not receive an
invitation to Sarah's birthday party, but her Sunday school teacher
tells her she should learn to forgive, like Jesus did.
        ISBN 0-7814-3241-3
        [1. Forgiveness—Fiction. 2. Christian life—Fiction.]
I. Title.
PZ7.S5884Mar 1999
[E] — dc21

                                                98-55699
                                                  CIP
                                                   AC

It isn't easy being Marpel on <u>any</u> day....

Her hair usually doesn't go right, she mostly says the wrong thing, and frankly, she doesn't really like herself very much.

Most of the time she acts like a show-off.

One day on the playground EVERYBODY in the class got an invitation to Sarah's party ...

...**everybody but Marpel.**

That made her feel pretty bad.

Sarah's parties were known throughout the town as the **most creative** and **fun parties** anywhere.

Last year she had a rodeo-themed birthday party with real ponies and an appearance from local country music legends Wes and Marilee Taggert.

When you feel sad and lonely, it's good to talk to a friend—someone who understands you . . .

. . . someone who will take the time to listen to your story.

So Marpel went to visit Gregory.

Since Gregory was too busy to listen, Marpel thought she'd go talk to Bradley and Tyler. They were older, so they would act more grown-up toward her.

It was obvious that Marpel wasn't going to get any help from her friends ...

... so she decided to take matters into her own hands.

This meant war.

Since Marpel wasn't invited to the party, she was gonna make sure **nobody** attended.

She'd rent a tractor and hide Sarah's whole house in some unknown mystery location.

Or maybe she should take a more subtle approach.

She could just vacuum up the entire party—cake and all—using the wet-dry vacuum that was in the garage.

Since Gregory, Bradley, and Tyler were all self-centered cootie boys, she'd take care of them later.

Perhaps some well-placed water balloons would get their attention.

All this revenge really can wear you out, even if it's just
in your imagination.

So Marpel decided to take a nap.

As is often the case, Marpel ended up dreaming about the things that were on her mind.

She dreamed she was the warden of a huge maximum-security prison. Guess who her prisoners were?

Sarah,

Gregory,

Bradley,

and Tyler.

And she rode them hard.

After the prisoners had their daily meal of cold liver and lima beans, Marpel was off to her office for her lunch of hamburgers, French fries, soft drink, and birthday cake.

But wait! Something was terribly wrong!

Marpel couldn't get out of the prison herself!!
She tried and tried, but nothing worked.

She was stuck in the prison . . .
just like everyone else.

Finally she awoke.

The dream gave Marpel the creeps, so she decided there was just one thing to do: go talk to Mrs. Fleece, her Sunday School teacher.

Mrs. Fleece seemed to know about this kind of thing . . . plus, she made the best peanut butter cookies in the world.

Mrs. Fleece was a good friend.

She welcomed Marpel into the house, offered her some warm cookies, and listened as Marpel shared about her hard day.

Everyone should have a friend like Mrs. Fleece—not
like stupid Gregory who was too busy riding his bike
to listen.

Oops.

Mrs. Fleece didn't let anyone call
anyone else stupid.

Marpel finally got to the part about the dream and the prison and not being able to get out. Mrs. Fleece kept her eyes on Marpel as she took a long sip of tea.

"Your dream is true," she said quietly.

Marpel was surprised.

She'd come here to feel better, but that hope was quickly slipping away.

Mrs. Fleece continued, "You see, whenever people hurt us and we don't forgive them, we've locked OURSELVES up just as we've locked them up."

"But they were mean to me," cried Marpel.

"Forgiving them doesn't mean that what they did wasn't wrong or that it didn't hurt," said Mrs. Fleece. "It means you've chosen not to still be mad about it."

"Did you know that **Jesus even forgave the people who nailed him to the cross?"**

As much as Marpel hated to admit it, something about what Mrs. Fleece said made sense.

Besides, where was Marpel gonna find a tractor big enough to move Sarah's whole house?

So Marpel decided to forgive Sarah and Gregory and Bradley and Tyler.

It took some practice.

As Marpel walked past the playground,
she spotted something stuck in the fence.

It was an envelope.

She opened it up.

Oh my! It was her invitation to Sarah's party. It must have blown away when Sarah was handing them out.

It had all been a simple mistake.

All the anger and thoughts of revenge had been a real waste of time and had just made Marpel miserable.

So Marpel went to Sarah's party. But it was Marpel who got the best present:

She had learned to forgive.

Faith Parenting Guide

Marpel Is Stuck!
And Other Really Good Reasons to Forgive

Age: 4-7

Life Issue: My child tends to hold grudges or doesn't apologize with sincerity.

Spiritual Building Block: Forgiveness

Learning Styles

Visual Learning Style: Ask your child to think of a time when she was angry at someone and held a grudge. Have her draw a picture of how she felt. Now ask her to think of a time when she forgave someone, and have her draw a picture of how that felt. Compare the pictures and ask her which felt better to her—forgiving someone or holding a grudge. Say: "Holding a grudge and being angry with someone might feel good at first, but after a while we feel stuck, just as Marpel did when she wouldn't forgive her friends."

Auditory Learning Style: Talk about Marpel's reasons for holding grudges against the other kids. Say: "It hurts when someone does something mean to us, like calling us names or not inviting us to a party. But holding a grudge and refusing to forgive others doesn't help. In fact, it just makes us feel worse inside." Now help your child think of ways to work out Marpel's problems with her classmates. If you can think of one, tell a story about a time you held a grudge against someone. Did you eventually forgive? What was the result of your forgiveness or unforgiveness? For example, was there a broken relationship?

Tactile Learning Style: Role-play the Parable of the Prodigal Son. (Keep it simple: Read the story in a children's Bible and let your kids dress up in sheets and bathrobes if you wish.) You play the prodigal and let your child play the father. (If you have more than one child, let each take a turn being the father.) Role-play in two ways the scene in which the prodigal returns: Have your child be unforgiving, then forgiving.

After each child has had a turn, discuss which felt better—forgiving the son or not forgiving him. If unforgiveness felt better, discuss how Marpel felt satisfaction while she was planning her revenge but began to feel that she was stuck in the prison of unforgiveness as time passed.

Help your child memorize a portion of Nehemiah 9:17: "But you are a forgiving God, gracious and compassionate, slow to anger and abounding in love" (NIV).